I0725099

Inklings Book 2025

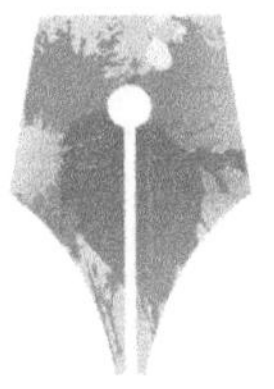

TEEN EDITION

The following youth authors contributed their short stories and poems to this anthology:

Advika Asthana

Yimeng Cai

Adele Coover

Zoë Friedman

Eleanor Frink-Davis

Raya Ilieva

Via M

William Manche

Kavya Murthy

Naomi Pond

Cover Design by Naomi Kinsman
Editorial Guidance by Naomi Kinsman & Tracy Piombo

Copyright © 2025, Society of Young Inklings (of the collection)
Copyright © of each work belongs to the respective author.
All rights reserved.
Printed in the USA
First printing: August 2025
ISBN: 978-1-956380-03-3

Contents

Thank you to our Collaborating Artists!

Julie Abe

John David Anderson

Kerry Aradhya

Kati Bartkowski

Rebecca Behrens

Ashley Herring Blake

Scott Bly

Dave Butler

Kacen Callender

Ernesto Cisneros

Kim Culbertson

Betty Culley

Jill Davis

Mandy Davis

Sharon M. Draper

Lisa Greenwald

Donna Barba Higuera

Marilyn Hilton

Joanna Ho

Ann Jacobus

Heidi Lang

Lea Lyon

Janae Marks

Beth McMullen

Patricia Newman

Daria Peoples

Mitali Perkins

Shannon Price

Helen Pyne

Caleb Smith

Laura Stegman

Raina Telgemeier

Ari Tison

Alder van Otterloo

Elizabeth Weiss Verdick

Ashley Walker

Pam Watts

Kristi Wright

Anne Young

Foreword

Welcome to the second annual Inklings Book: Teen Edition. Since 2008, Society of Young Inklings has invited youth writers to submit their stories and poems to the Inklings Book Contest, with the chance to be featured in our yearly anthology. For many years, those anthologies included writers from 3rd–9th grade. As our community grew, so did our circle of dedicated teen writers, and we are delighted to celebrate their unique voices once again in this edition created especially for them.

One of the hallmarks of the Inklings Book Contest is the opportunity to experience a professional editorial process before publication. In the main anthology, young authors work alongside adult mentors. In the *Teen Edition*, however, we designed a peer-to-peer model, inviting our teen writers to serve as editors for one another. Together, they highlighted what was most powerful in each piece, then offered suggestions to help the author pursue their chosen revision focus.

There's something invigorating about engaging with a community of writers who care as much about words as you do. When another writer asks, "What else might this piece become?" it opens doors you might not have noticed alone. In the interviews ahead, you'll hear from these authors about the possibilities they discovered as they revised through that lens of curiosity and collaboration.

The works gathered here—ten poems and stories by high school writers—brim with honesty, resilience, and daring imagination. You'll encounter themes of love, betrayal, hope, and resilience, each piece offering its own insight and inspiration. Most of all, you'll hear these young writers urging you to recognize the strength of your own voice and to share it boldly.

If you'd like to learn more about becoming an Inkling, visit us at younginklings.org. There, you'll find writing prompts, interviews, membership opportunities, and details about how you can participate in future contests. We're so glad you've joined us for this celebration of teen voices.

With gratitude,
Naomi Kinsman
Founder, Society of Young Inklings

Taste Buds

by Advika Asthana

Life
Dances on the tongue.
Each taste an echo
layered, unexpected,
pungent, mellow,
nuanced.

Sweet
Like golden honey
packed with the bright light of the sun,
and creamy frosting
bliss that feels too good to let go.
Like when my grandfather cut fruits and
we sunk our teeth into watermelon.
We played for hours on the roof
under the golden hues of the sky
our smiles carved into our cheeks.

Salty

Like the brine of olive juice

that picks at your taste buds.

Like feeling each individual salt grain

that coated a warm pretzel,

leaving traces of acid on your teeth.

Like when he smirked and told me

he did better on the test

and my heart sank further

and I plastered a smile

hiding the ache of his success.

Sour

Like your lips sucked in

recoiling at the sharp sting of lemon,

or the fierce smell of vinegar

when it floats up your nose

and near sears each hair off.

Like when she laughed and made

that same comment about my size.

I stood stupidly with my cheeks burning

trying not to turn red

and praying my face wouldn't

betray me.

Bitter
Like when the drops of black coffee
that bite at the back of your tongue
linger in your mouth.
Even after trying to wash it out multiple times,
tingling repeatedly when you
tried to forget.
Like when I reread the rejection letter over
and over
and over again.
Isn't that why it's called
the bitter truth?

Taste buds
Balanced on the tip of the tongue
feeling each and every of the
sweet, salty, sour, and bitter.
Not every bite delights
yet it makes the feast whole,
and worth remembering.

Advika Asthana

– Author Interview

Advika Asthana is a ninth-grade student passionate about writing. She has several poems and short prose pieces published in local magazines. When she's not writing, she enjoys listening to music and watching movies. She hopes to continue growing as a young writer.

What surprised you about the revision process?

Working with my writing peers, my poem became something different and went in directions I didn't originally think of. This revision process was also unique to other processes I'd done before. We first selected a focus and then edited specifically on that focus instead of just doing a general revision. What I loved about this is that one specific aspect of our pieces became so much better. For me, my focus was something I felt like I was lacking. By focusing on that specific aspect, I could bring the poem to levels I didn't even consider in the first draft.

How has your piece developed from your first draft?

My main change was that I played around with the structure. With the help of my peers, I changed up the punctuation. I loved how those changes elevated my piece. The thoughts and feelings I was conveying stayed the same, but instead of being one long sentence, each idea was emphasized and developed. I also turned the poem into a more cohesive narrative, tying it all together instead of isolating each different taste. Surprisingly, I got a message out of this revision which was important to me. At first, I had written the poem from a random idea of equating feelings to tastes, but I love that it became something more meaningful.

How did the people and feedback shape your final piece?

Each person who looked over my poem played a vital role in bringing it to the version it is today. Their thoughtful feedback and fresh perspectives are what helped me see the piece in new ways, bring out its message, and refine its voice. Before sharing it, I didn't fully consider elements like structure, punctuation, and theme. Through the insights of those who viewed the poem, I was able to see it as a cohesive narrative. Their comments generally pushed me to think critically of how several different elements can elevate the poem.

How did you first get into writing, and why poetry?

I remember first doing a writing challenge in elementary, where I wrote a little rhyming poem. My friends and parents loved it, and pushed me to do a little more writing. As I wrote more, it became something I used to express thoughts into something meaningful. It can sort through feelings, mesh experiences, anything. I fell in love with poetry because it can be both structured and random, and do everything I look for in writing. Over time, I realized that poetry wasn't just something I liked, but also was something I needed to divert my mind. It gives me a way to express through imagery what might be difficult to say verbally.

Why do you love writing?

Writing to me is more than just putting down words; it's an outlet, a space where I can explore people, places, and emotions that matter. I'm drawn to the idea that writing carries messages, which might be subtle or in-your-face loud. I always hope with anything I write is that readers will both learn something and feel something, and that my words resonate beyond just the page. I've been able to share my inner world with others through writing and have discovered how powerful language can be.

Potential Energy

by Raya Ilieva

In the studio, there is a sticky, heady sense of delirium: air trapped too long and perfumed with early-evening sunlight. Even with a glass window exhibiting us to the outside, I feel confined. In front of me, Asya crooks her neck left, her pointe shoe tapping the sticky floor. It's musically precise but not mechanically so; I count the off-beats in my head. Ms. Yana taps Asya's neck with the wooden pointer, harsh. She'd be gentler, but Asya's had this concentration habit for years.

We all know how hard it is to break a habit—it just seems easier when it's not yours. I watch Asya breathe in laborious exhales. Her ankles are shaking; tiny tremors run up her calves, and her head's started drifting sideways again. The muscle in my leg cramps and spasms trying to follow her technique, right as Ms. Yana clicks off the music. The wingbeats of our movements stop, and the room is less dense.

I stumble through the *reverence* and hobble to the corner, so I can rub a finger over the spot on my leg, still tense. Asya folds her long legs under her as her fingers find the swell on her neck that's developed over years of Ms. Yana tapping the spot. It's not the first time, but the bruise has bloomed to a fuchsia. I don't say anything. I just watch her slide on a turtleneck and arrange her light-colored hair around the spot, which is still slightly visible. I feel a stab of pity; the neck is a hard one to hide.

Outside, the sky rolls belly-up above me. It bawls out green and pink that turn the deep blue neon and grotesque, and I remember hearing that the brighter the sunset, the more thickly polluted the area. I'm not surprised; even the streetlamps seem to ooze chemicals. Their white glow is resigned, submissive.

The walk to the train station pulls at my muscles. My own bruises—ghoulishly green—are on my ankles, for the way they wobble up high. I can always feel them, and even not directly touched, they darken and pulse, like they want to break out of my skin, for which I don't blame them. On the train, I draw my knees into my chest and my fingers compulsively find the spot and press down. Other girls have it worse! I tell myself. Even as littles, first learning, in our pristine pink tights, how to do what we were told, an order presented itself; certain girls were corrected more than others, certain ones have had their defects viciously pointed out to them since they were seven. At least when I was small, I held the illusion that I was liked. I think of Asya, drawing her sweater around herself. It hides her body, too, and I know she's gotten warnings about her weight though she's as skinny as the rest of us.

The train hisses and slows; I unfold myself and disembark. I hate the walk back home, especially at night, when pools of sound gather in the gaps between wind bursts, and the oil on the ground by the auto shop gleams and smells rancid. Inside, the only light comes from my father's computer as it ghoulishly swims over his features. The door slams behind me. My father stirs, but only to drag a hand down the side of his face and click his mouse. Once I'm in bed, he plods down the hall to his bedroom, stopping outside my door. For a second I think he's going to do something, but he doesn't, just pauses and moves on.

At ballet the next day, Asya sits next to me on my usual corner bench. She says nothing, winding her flaxy hair into a high bun. I bend down and focus on the neat roll of waxy tape I slide over my blisters, followed by the toepads, tights, shoes. Warmups I always do holding onto a wall, rising metronomically up and down. But Asya stretches slowly, legs forming an easy one-hundred-and-eighty degrees. She bends backward and I wince. Extensions used to be my specialty; a few months ago, I was as elastic as a rubber children's toy.

I was first for some weeks, before the pain started. Small eruptions that felt as if something mysterious was taking control of me one vertebrae at a time. How many weeks? One, two. Never more. The list is posted on the main bulletin board, one for each of Ms. Yana's classes. We are the oldest, always permitted to look first and linger.

That day was in March, 60-something outside with thin ribbons of wind. I had lost a bit of weight, somehow, and there I was, bony and proud to see my name scratched almost illegibly: 1) Klara M. Smiling, among the hisses of the other girls.

I locked myself in the bathroom, only to count my ribs and tell myself there must have been something to like in my peeling skin and awkward joints if I was first on the list. Favorite—leader—and then just as soon I wasn't. The euphoria dripped away; I noticed the way my ankles shot bolts of pain up my legs to my hips, and Ms. Yana noticed too.

It was a fluke, my body told me. I gained all the weight back and more. Crammed food into my mouth at every hour and watched with sick fascination the purple scars on my thighs stretch and grow as my name slid down the list. Now there's barely any heart in any of it: the practice, the rituals, the list. I had my chance and I blew it; so what now. I watch with a strange confusion the dedication the other girls put into this. How stubbornly they believe that if they can only get a higher arabesque or arch their backs even more or reach oblivion, they will be loved. How stubbornly I used to believe the same. How happy I was, believing, swallowing every pain, treading on.

Asya is a consistent fourth, though in my mind, she should be higher. There's a sinuous quality to her dancing, a tugging elasticity that comes from somewhere beyond reach. Like she pours something into the floor, changing its color just slightly. She's a bullet of potential energy waiting to be fired.

Ms. Yana's style, though, is more airy and empty. She teaches the other girls to strive for conformity and sharp angles. A herd of them moves all the same, pink tights blending into black leotards into high buns. Ms. Yana calls them beautiful. Somehow they've cracked the code to passionless, technical dancing.

They're not the same, and they are skilled, very. But when I watch them, all I feel is a weighted deadening of my soul, not the thrumming anticipation that is Asya's dancing: all clean, strong lines from her willowy body. I wish Ms. Yana would open her eyes and see.

The pain becomes overwhelming. I take two days off, even though it feels like severing one of my fingers. I barely remember them: a haze of eating and numbness. My father, passing by me on the way to his study, asked, confused and a little hurt, why I was not at ballet. His accusation surprised me: I realized that he used to take me to the studio and watch me have class, even twisting together my buns with his large fingers and clumsily sewing elastics onto my shoes, but the memory was so old I could barely picture it clearly anymore.

When he realized that it was not just a sweet, passing phase, that I was throwing my whole body into it with determined unrestraint, he withdrew. I stopped complaining about aches and worries, knowing he would only stare at me with confused resentment. Injured, though, with the possibility of my quitting hanging in the air—although I would never speak it into being—I could feel him wondering *why*, to which I offered no answer.

In any case, the air is a little different when I return, sharper, pointier. Ms. Yana doesn't ask if I feel better, so I don't tell her that I am worse, or that I feel as if I have become weak and soft, and every word and sound hurts my limbs.

No one pays me any attention at all. At the barre, my sweaty palm clings to the wood, and my muscles feel atrophied, core weakened, thighs aching. Asya is still in front of me, though I seem to be endlessly bigger than her, like she is a delicate child and I the tired and softened mother. Her head is tilted more than usual and her movements are ferocious, primal. Her back muscles expand and contract like wings as her arms move. She flicks her head back to me once, and the harshness of her eyes and jaw stuns me, as if there is a mountain of energy waiting behind her stare. I resist the urge to ask, what happened?

After class, on the ailing benches, I try to knead my fingers into the knots of pain at my hips. It doesn't work, and because I want to delay my individual practice, I trek to the bathrooms in the back. Right by them is a glass door, and though the lights inside warp my view, I see a figure out in the darkness. I step outside, away from the stuffy hallway, and see that the apparition is Asya.

She holds a phone close to her ear and keens into it, sobbing in gargled cries. I freeze in my spot, mouth half-open, and try to decipher what she's saying before realizing it's in another language. She shouts something final, then jams her finger into the screen and sends her phone skidding across the pavement. I gasp as it skitters to a stop but Asya doesn't react because she's now screaming into the darkened alleyway, the force of it animalistic and gutted.

I stay still until she wears herself out and only hiccups occasionally, like a baby crying itself to sleep; then turns and, seeing me, opens her mouth in a wordless O, eyes flashing wide and glistening. My chest heaves in time with hers as we stare at each other until I gulp and back away, slowly, inside.

On the ride home, my heart won't stop clattering in my chest. In the grimy yellow windows of the train, Asya's face shudders over and over again. Her arms gesticulate, she swivels around, her mouth opens at me. Arms, turn, mouth. And again, again, like one of Ms. Yana's nightmare combinations in the center. Repeat, repeat. Come here. You are wrong, like this instead. Okay. Again.

When I fall, Asya is the only one who stops moving, seemingly more as a reflex than a genuine desire to help. I'm caught speechless with the sheer pain and excruciating shock of it all, my ankles, hips, knees, everything. But I see her, out of the corner of my eye.

She bends down next to me. "Are you—"

"Az." Ms. Yana has heaved herself creakily out of the tall, ancient chair she perches in. She pulls Asya away from me almost protectively, as if I am a disease. "Keep going, I take care of it."

I feel Asya slink away. Near me, pointe shoes hit the floor like children's blocks. Cheerful, rote piano music spills into the room, near my head. Salt flows from my eyes, dribbling down my face.

I haven't seen the floor so close—gray Marley vinyl, slashed with black streaks and dusted by grit—since I fell years ago, slipped out of a pirouette. At that point I was still in love with ballet and my growth spurt, the beginning of the end, hadn't yet attacked me. It was the first level where our classes were taught by Ms. Yana: before, she had been a spectral presence, someone the older girls spoke of with terrified reverence, and we were taught by the stern but warmhearted Ms. Sofia, but come age eleven, every afternoon we faced the hunched old woman, and she re-taught us everything we knew about work, about striving, about listening and following.

I remember that first fall clearly; I can see the early-spring light and feel my shock at my body, for it having betrayed me. I remember hands, reaching towards me, small and soft like my own: our pack of girls was not so divided then. I remember an admonishment, a flush of shame, my heart surging from adrenaline. I do not seem to remember the pain.

Now, everything is different. I am crying and disgusting for it. Ms. Yana can barely stoop towards me. She is so, so old.

"You can stand?"

I try, heaving unattractive breaths, but the sheer agony that crushes my hip makes me crumble down again. "I can't—"

An infinity later, I'm scrabbling for the barre. The other girls have finally stopped, and as I stagger to the door, I wait for Ms. Yana to yell at them. But no, she's leading me out to the benches in the lobby, and I'm crying, clutching blindly at my hip through the haze and pain, and here my teacher of seven years is asking me what happened, Klara?

My throat feels blocked when I bawl, "I think it's broken."

She just sighs and glances at me. "I get back to class. You wait."

A phone call and she's gone.

Half an hour passes. I slump—half sitting, half lying down—on these horrible benches, contorted where she left me. If I try to move, something hurts in bright, deep pain: my sores bleeding through my shoes; my left foot hanging limply from the ankle, which is bent out of balletic alignment; both knees shaking and spilling bruises from breaking my fall; and my hips. The one I landed sideways on feels shattered, and if I try to move it, it explodes in earthsplitting pain.

Class lets out and the shame rolls in, crawling into my ribs. A few girls come over and attempt conversation, but I turn my head to the wall until they leave and cold skin is suddenly brushing my face.

Asya. Again. I don't push her away when she clamps my wrist in her long, skeletal fingers. I'm still crying, so I try to stifle it with all manner of choked and hacking sobs, grotesque noises, really, until Asya finally, finally speaks.

"Cry," she says. "Okay. It's . . ." She cuts herself off, which I appreciate.

She knows, better than anyone, how spectacularly not okay it is. A bone is broken, maybe multiple. This could be career-ending, not that we can call this meaningless, endless work in the studio every day a career anyway. My soft, innocent hidden heart—my baby self—is devastated and shocked. My current body, husk that it is, knew it was coming someday, but still manages to be sadly aghast.

She knows, so she says nothing. But the hot, red mess that is my face stays turned up to the mildewing ceiling, growing more flushed and feverish by the minute. Same girl, I remember, who a week ago was screaming into the darkness. Now she's placing her knuckles, gently, on my cheek and smoothing out my tears, blurring them into my skin, saying something as she leans towards me, those gray eyes so full of concern: "Klara, I—" And then the door swings open and my father is stepping in and seeing me and coming over defeatedly to carry me outside and Asya is gone again.

"Broken *hip*," says the doctor. "At fifteen. Can you believe it."

"Oh, gosh, no," says the nurse, touching his arm. "So sad."

"Dancer, too. That's what the dad said."

"Oh my gosh. So sad."

My days are spent woozy on pain meds and wrapped in plaster. I see more of Dad than I ever did before, it seems; he is over frequently, signing papers, talking in a tired voice to the nurses. He sits by my bed sometimes, when he thinks I'm asleep, looking burdened.

I'm always alone at night: Dad leaves, the nurses leave, everyone leaves. But it's night when a face appears at my doorway, then a body with the gnarled old hands of Ms. Yana. I'm sitting up, awake, and my heart stutters when I see her.

She's dressed exactly as I've always known her: wide black pants, thick sweater, a chunky beaded necklace, and a tight, wiry ponytail. She looks deeply out of place without hordes of ballerinas around her, exuding less force now that she's not leeching off a wellspring of it.

I want to flee, but I'm trapped amid a messy tangle of wires and sheets. Ms. Yana clears her throat, but her voice still cracks when she says my name. I've memorized the way the bitter syllables fall from her lips, and the words that come after are, too, not unfamiliar.

Taking too long to recover. Skills were degrading anyway. Not the level of commitment required. Won't be allowed to continue even after recovery. Sorry. And there's really nothing I can do but listen to her silently, say okay when she's done, and watch her leave, walking crookedly.

I think I fall asleep after, just sitting numbly in my bed: not with denial, just a quiet affirmation of the truth I already knew, that ballet had long since shut me out of its sphere.

Dad doesn't trust himself to care for me at home while I'm mostly immobilized, so he asks if I can stay in the hospital for extra time. I quickly get used to it, and even to the pain, the familiar fog it provides coupled with the fuzziness of the meds.

I don't want visitors, not after Ms. Yana's blow. But I have time to wonder what she's told the ballet girls about me, or if they miss me—at least a little? Maybe? Probably not, so when Dad tells me I have a girl here to see me, "a ballerina?" he says hesitantly, I laugh. But no, no, she really is, he says, here for you. Do you know another Klara M. with a broken hip, hmm?

Okay, fine, I say, unconvinced. He goes away. Minutes pass. I doubt he is correct in his assumption. I close my eyes, try to drift off into a nap, but wait, there's a light knock. I startle up. At first, just a hand: long, white, thin. Smooth. Asya? But why—

Yes, it is her, stepping gingerly and fluidly into the room. It's November and the light that washes in through the window is smooth and gray. Asya's in clearer focus than I've ever seen her, wrapped in a thin, long-sleeved sweater that only accentuates her birdlike slimness. Her hair is falling in soft, pale waves around her face, barely covering the ghostlike shadow of a bruise on her neck, and in leggings and the sweater with her gray eyes staring at me, she's like a jewel, so delicately wrought and deliberate, perfect in the middle of the hospital.

She perches on the plastic chair, still angelic, still unbelievable. "I'm sorry," she says. Her voice is low and smooth, a slightly accented hum.

"Why?" A whisper, barely a question.

"I didn't . . . didn't do enough. You're gone."

"You didn't . . . Asya . . . no, I—"

"I think . . . I'm going to quit? I don't know. I don't know why I had to tell you."

"No, Asya, no." My heart splinters; a valve breaks off. The thought of her never dancing again wrenches me apart. She was born to flash and leap and swoop and kick with muscular energy.

She looks so sad and small, and I realize what I've done: put her in a box, just like Ms. Yana did. "But you should, if you want to."

"Yeah, well, I . . . It's worse, you don't know. Something's off—in her teaching, she's vicious, even more so."

I smile sadly at her. "There was always something off there."

"Yes." She nods. "Yes."

"But?"

"But it's worse, and I'm sorry."

I study her then, this morose, beautiful girl, chin in her hands in front of me, and see the fatigue built up in her eyes and the aching lethargy in her limbs. I watch the years tick by and chisel her features into something isolated, on display. I glance at every perfectly-formed half-moon nail and arching muscle and her skin slotted neatly over her frame. Everything inside collected into one vessel, sadness piling up into girl as leaves skitter and toss silently outside. And what is there to do but take her hand, all of it, gently, in my own and listen to the pulse between us? To tell ourselves, quietly, that we can exist without ballet, that there's still energy inside that belongs to us, coiled and waiting to be spent.

Raya Ilieva
– Author Interview

Raya Ilieva is a fifteen-year-old writer living in the San Francisco Bay Area. She is a sophomore at The Nueva School and is on the editorial boards of the Nueva literary magazine and scholarly journal. Her work has been recognized by the Scholastic Art and Writing Awards and the Society of Young Inklings, and she self-published a novella at ten years old and a short story collection in her eighth grade year. She loves to read and write realistic fiction and short stories, and when not thinking about words, she can be found dancing, listening to music, or hiking.

What authors inspire you?

I love reading authors who are obsessed with language, and whose work is worth reading for the prose as much as the story. Jhumpa Lahiri, Virginia Woolf, and Claire Keegan are three of my favorites for this reason: each of their sentences, in different ways, is exquisitely crafted, with not a word out of place, and their writing is extraordinarily beautiful without being overwrought or clichéd.

What advice do you have for other youth writers?

Read as much as you can and write as much as you can. Although it's tempting to lock yourself into one style or mode of expression because you think you are "good at it," or only read the genre which you enjoy the most, exposing yourself to a wide range of writers—from all kinds of time periods and backgrounds—and absorbing their voices will help you find a more authentic voice of your own, and it makes the whole process of writing so much more interesting. At least in my experience, reading and writing a lot are pretty much the only ways to get any better!

What was the revision process like for you?

Revising my story with Inklings was very interesting, because I had gone over it many times before, both on my own and with other people's feedback. Getting the chance to revisit the story a year and a half after it was written and get notes from my peers and my mentor made me reconsider it in a new light. Although I didn't change it drastically, the edits I did make convinced me that nothing is ever truly finished and there's always more to improve.

What inspired this piece?

I've been a competitive ballroom (also known as dancesport) dancer for over nine years, and I also danced ballet for several years. Growing up in the dance world has made it something I know closely, and the challenge of describing physical movement in words has always fascinated me. *Potential Energy* arose from my love for dance and the many long hours I've spent in the studio. However, it's worth nothing that it is highly dramatized and I have not personally experienced anything like the events described in the story.

How did you approach writing *Potential Energy*?

I had no plan or outline whatsoever, only an impression about the setting and a vague idea of the main character in my head. Then I just began writing, discovering the story as I went. I wrote it out of order, and then put the sections together and added some connective transitions. I usually write in this way, preferring to follow the story as it naturally arises instead of forcing what I think it will be.

Morning

by Adele Coover

Waves lapped gently on the sandy shore, a steady rhythm in the otherwise quiet night. It was the witching hour, a time where most were asleep, but those who were not, waited calmly for the sun to rise and push back the mist that covered the bay. On a pier, sat a young boy, next to him, a heron. Together they observed as the water drew in, then out. As the boy looked through the darkness, he could faintly see himself in the water. Skin: sallow and pale; eyes: hollow and dark. Lips blue, hair wet. His reflection stared up at the sky, as he stared down at the sea.

The heron sat patiently, wings folded back, eyes gently following the child. The boy did not move, nor speak, nor even blink. A boy who, hours earlier bounced around restlessly; running up and down the crowded pier. People from all over the world walked on the wooden planks, enjoying the sunny day. Food carts and souvenir stands everywhere, calling for attention, broadcasted their ripe fruit and handwoven hats. Yellows, pinks and reds. Sunshine, toys, candy and clothes. Music and laughter, rich smells and sweet treats. A little boy's playground, safe and bright; disrupted by one, small shove. Maybe it was intentional; but probably not. Just too many people at the same place, at the same time, quickly moving from one distraction to another. One small push, just a little nudge, that sent a child tumbling down, off the pier and into the air. A free fall, down, down, down. No time to contemplate the meaning, only a moment to realize that the colorful stalls had been left behind, until slamming into a hard surface. Boy splashing and ocean engulfing. A pained gasp was let out and as air escaped, salt water reached in. Water that holds one down and fills the lungs. That sends little arms and legs beating frantically, but, where to go? No up, nor down; just salt and water. Overwhelming and controlling. Water that does not soothe, nor cool one down; instead creates panic in the brain and sets a roaring fire ablaze in the lungs. A fire that spread throughout the body; vitalizing but deadly. Painful and invigorating. A desperate fight. Frantic hands failing out as water beacons, dragging one down. Then. Finally. Something solid. The fight had ended, the burning ceased, the moving stopped, the calm returned.

On the pier sat a boy and a heron. As the sun rose and the mist receded, leaving behind nothing but sparkling droplets, the heron took off. His great wings flapped, following the moon's retreat, always in the realm of dreams. In the pale morning light, under the pier, lay the body of a boy, with hands splintered and bleeding, waves slowly pushing him, back and forth.

Adele Coover

– Author Interview

Adele Coover is a high schooler in Philadelphia, who has not participated in any writing competitions outside of one Nanowrimo competition five years ago. Though Adele has been inventing stories from a very young age, this did not include a desire to read nor write till the age of ten. Instead, Adele did many other activities like soccer, circus and art. The art factor is an important part of the creative process, and Adele still spends a lot of time drawing to map out characters and important plot points. Adele also rock climbs and does theater which are also both good conduits for energy not spent writing.

Adele was recently in a production of the Shakespeare play *Twelfth Night* and played as a priest and a servant. Both characters but mostly the priest have the role of creating chaos while explaining an event that has happened off stage. Adele is a student with a lot of creativity who loves stories and writing as well as art and theater.

Why do you enjoy writing?

Ever since I started I have always found writing calming even when writing a scene with a lot of action and strong emotions. My love for stories transports me to a place in my mind that I really love. My creativity has always been with me and writing allows me to express it. There are so many stories that exist and my brain overflows with them. I don't always write them down, in fact I rarely do, but when I sit down and transcribe what's in my brain, I feel at peace. Writing is a gateway out of my mind that allows me to share what I value the most about myself, my stories.

What books/authors inspired you?

I always loved books in verse, so books like *The Poet X* and *A Long Way Down* have influenced my writing style, even in prose. Though overall, for my passion for writing, and especially with a slight fantastical element to it, I would attribute it to Rick Riordan. His books got me into reading and later into mythology and older stories, and that inspires my own. In conclusion, mythological stories and the entire fantasy genre inspire me to write, while poetry and stories in verse influence the way my stories flow.

What advice would you give younger authors?

I think that finding people to read your work is important. It is always nice to have constructive feedback to better the piece. Also having someone look over your work can feel really validating. Even for stories that you are not ready to share with strangers, finding people you are close to and having them read it can give tangibility to your work. That being said, there is no need to follow the advice that is given to. Every one has stylistic preferences so if someone gives you advice that you do not think contributes or you think changes the style too much, don't sweat it. Everyone has their own unique style and that is what matters.

What are you writing now?

I am currently in the midst of writing two different stories. One of them is a satire on musicals that take place in high school, specifically the darker ones like *Heathers* or *Carrie: The Musical.* It follows two jocks as they struggle between being the top of the high school food chain and being themselves. The other story is a story in verse that takes place in a giant circus-like dystopian place that the main character is trying to escape. He ends up there by accident, where he is aided by a puppet who is really bored and desires to be his friend. Neither story has progressed very far, but I am working on them.

Bum-bum-bum-bum-bum-bum-buuuum

by William Manche

Ever since I was a little kid, I have been obsessed with
sports chants.
The resounding sound of thousands of voices echoing together,
"bum-bum-bum-bum-bum-buuuum."
My mood changes.
Brightly colorful crowds change as the glorious game of football shifts,
from the sweet roar of triumph to the bitter sting of defeat.
I swing with them, up and down, like a wave rising and falling.

They are my heart and soul,
Fueling me through days.
I hum their simple, irresistible tune,
"bum-bum-bum-bum-bum-buuuum."

Chilly fever in the air,

My first Michigan football game.

Waves of people pouring through entrances,

The scent of buttery popcorn and sweat mixed with the crisp autumn breeze.

A sold-out stadium roars around me,

A living sea of sound.

Yellow stretches out as far as my eye can see,

Shirts, towels, flags, and foam fingers waving in the electric air.

At kickoff, the greatest chant I had ever heard-

"Bum-bum-bum-bum-bum-buuuum."

Millions and millions of flags flowing like water,

The thunder of the Seven Nation Army chant rolling through the crowd.

"Bum-bum-bum-bum-bum-buuuum."

The chant struck like lightning inside my heart,

A spark, then fire,

Burning brighter with every beat,

Filling my heart with spirit and euphoria.

The football screams through the air,

It waves bye to the defender as it lands in the receiver's hands.

The crowd ignites as one,

A roaring blaze of sound and motion.

Exhilarated by the crowd's energy and intensity,

My heart burns with fire,

My heart pounding in rhythm with the passion of the crowd.

I feel a sense of camaraderie among even strangers,
There is nothing as magical as a Michigan football game.
The chant brings people together,
It unites them as the crowd becomes one.
Surging together like the great swell of ocean waves,
"Bum-bum-bum-bum-bum-buuuum."

William Manche

– Author Interview

William Manche is a 10th grader at Los Altos High School who loves writing, reading, and playing/watching sports. Writing gives him a way to share my thoughts and experiences, especially his passion for sports. He enjoys bringing others into the game through words, capturing the strategy, teamwork, and focus that make it so special to him. He typically doesn't write poems, but he chose this genre to share his experience and emotions at sporting events. He wants to continue writing poems as another way to express himself creatively and reflect on his experiences. He enjoys reading, especially dystopian fiction. He likes the thrill of excitement they give him, as he is captured by the intense moments throughout dystopian novels. William is drawn to stories about resilience and justice, and appreciates how they make him think critically about the world. No matter where he is—at school, in sports, or his community—he tries to stay engaged, work hard, and make a positive impact. He looks forward to continuing to grow as a writer.

Why do you enjoy writing?

I enjoy writing because it gives me a way to create my world and share stories and ideas that matter to me. Sometimes I have ideas or feelings that are hard to explain out loud, but writing gives me a way to express them more clearly.

It also pushes me to be more creative and explore different perspectives. Writing also pushes me to be more creative. Whether I'm working on a poem, a personal reflection, or a story, I get to experiment with language, structure, and emotion. Writing helps me visualize my ideas and makes me feel like my thoughts and emotions have a place to go. When I write, it's like turning something abstract into something real—I can see my thoughts take shape on the page. Writing gives me a sense of clarity and creativity that aren't always easy to express out loud.

What are some of your favorite books or authors?

I enjoy reading dystopian genre books because of the fast-paced plots and high-stakes worlds, which makes the books hard to put down. I like how *The Hunger Games*, *The Maze Runner*, *Ready Player One*, and *Divergent* all take place in high-stakes worlds where characters are forced to challenge unfair systems and discover who they truly are. These themes keep the stories exciting while also making me think about real-world issues.

What feeling did you hope to create with your poem? What poetic strategies did you use to create that feeling?

I wanted to create a feeling of excitement and unity, like you're in the middle of the stadium, surrounded by a sea of fans chanting together. The poem captures the energy, pride, and enthusiasm of being at a Michigan football game. I used hyperboles, sensory details, and imagery to create the electric atmosphere of game day and make the reader feel like they were in the moment. I used hyperboles to exaggerate the intensity of the crowd, like "a living sea of sound," to show how powerful the atmosphere felt. I also used sensory details, like the smell of buttery popcorn, bright yellow in every direction, and the roar of the crowd, to immerse the reader in the moment. Vivid imagery allowed me to paint a mental picture of the stadium coming alive. I also used repetition in key lines to mirror the crowd's chants and create a rhythmic energy that reflects the pulse of the game. Overall, I wanted the poem to help others understand the powerful spirit of game day.

How do you choose your words and images?

I used vivid images like the roar of the stadium to help readers picture the moment and feel the excitement. I also tried to use a lot of poetic devices to capture the energy of the crowd. I wanted the language to be rhythmic, as if you could hear the chants throughout the poem. I believed that the more poetic devices I used, the stronger the poem's impact would be on the reader. I love using tools like imagery, metaphor, alliteration, and rhythm to bring emotion and meaning to life. These tools help me focus on my overall goal as a writer: to make every word matter. I started thinking this way in English class this year, when we were challenged to focus on our word choice in our pieces of writing. To this day, it has stuck with me. I have continued to focus on intentional language, and it's helped me write with more clarity, purpose, and impact across everything I create.

fog

by Kavya Murthy

Fog, settling over the tops of trees and melting down through the sky like spiderwebs draped across forested hills.

Lines of trees trapped by fences as they lurch and lean and pitch their branches over the highways, reaching, reaching.

The valleyed body of mother Earth with the scars and folds of her rolling stomach, the creases where water once screamed in racing rivulets, century after century, taking, folding, pinching.

But there is beauty in our destruction too, in the litter of plastic buildings built on stolen dirt, there is beauty in the clusters of boxes that dig their nails and scrape through the land.

We dig down, down, with grubby hands and oil drills- like vultures- our skin browned with dirt as we ravage you for things to steal and call our own.

Buildings climb up, up, up, faster than the trees, grandeur and splendor rich off the blood of all that died for them- we can't fathom you, you that brings life again from the old dead, from mushrooms who creep into the ground to turn the wheel and begin anew.

Our highways spin and curve in twisted mimicry of the raging waters that could have been, furious torrents that could still be, dipping and rising and coughing as the fuel hits your throat.

We rid our nights of constellations, they are not bright enough- we fill the darkness instead with the hazy chemical glow of street lamps, looming shadows and neon fluorescence and city lights that never sleep until we blot out so many stars we forget what they looked like at all.

Vast plains of flat rippling water interrupted by ships belching fat clouds; we slice through your volumes with bridges that grab your clouds in angry fistfuls and pull the sky to the ground because you are too perfect to leave alone and you must be destroyed.

We tie ropes around your wrists and the friction of the wheels leaves burnt scars in their wake, we run our hands through your hair in gentle caress and then grab and pull till you scream and punch and kick and cry and even then we don't stop.

We make beauty in our destruction, in our concrete jungles, our picket white fences, so we can suspend our own disbelief- so that we don't feel each wound we inflict upon you.

We make beauty in our destruction so that we can pretend that it's okay.

42

We climb and we kill and we purge and destroy but we don't stop.

Kavya Murthy

– Author Interview

Kavya Murthy is a rising junior at Mountain View High School, California. She started writing songs and poetry in elementary school, but only really started considering herself a "poet" around eighth grade. This year's Inklings Book Contest was her first opportunity to interact with the Inklings community, and she's so glad to have done so. Outside of writing, she plays viola and is interested in psychology.

What inspired this piece?

This piece came to me on a drive up to San Francisco. I had been trying out this new thing, where I write little fragments of imagery just to "exercise the muscle"—that's where the first line came from, looking out the window and just writing something down. I really wasn't expecting it to be as long or as coherent as it ended up being, but the story kept unfolding as we moved along: the hills, the blocky cities, the Bay Bridge across the water.

What does "there is beauty in our destruction" mean?

This was an idea I had been untangling before this poem began. Seeing just how much of the world we have changed irreparably inspires some kind of loathing in me—but even then, I can't help but appreciate the extent of it, the sheer enormity. The simple fact that we can do such things—literally scrape the sky—is staggering. Appalling, but still somehow beautiful.

What was the editorial process like?

I have never had the opportunity before to work so closely with others my age passionate about the same thing, and it was truly a welcome experience. In fact, I have never really attempted to revise *any* poem I've made, afraid it might ruin some sense of authenticity. While I think it does depend on the poem, I don't feel that happened here. By far the most helpful tip I have is to space out your revision work—each time you come back to it, lines that started out feeling clunky slowly meld into the rest of the work, becoming part of the whole.

Chiaroscuro

by Yimeng Cai

Art.

What was it?

It was the splattering of paint onto an empty canvas. It was watching ceruleans and ametrines and slates swirl into a pieced-together work. It was smearing blotches of acrylic to create shapes beyond one's comprehension. It was that quiet swell in his chest whenever he finished a piece.

To him, art was more than an expression—it was freedom. He found a sort of comfort within each and every stroke—whether it be as gentle as the spring breeze or as turbulent as the turning sea. He could distract himself with his overgrown evergreens, get lost within the reds and oranges and pinks of his fading sunsets—trapping himself within his painted landscapes to gain a sense of control…

Through art, he could escape the world others called reality.

Or at least, that was what he thought. When he had first packed up his bags—when he had finally said his bitter farewells to the scornful eyes of family—he had thought he was free. How could he not? He was finally out of that wretched home. He would never have to see expectant Mother, always-busy Father, or his siblings—outshining him in anything and everything—ever again.

He could be enough, he thought. He would finally be enough.

Oh, how he was wrong.

The young man dragged himself across his studio floor—his dandruff-infested locks and eerily thin figure almost as unsettling as the background. He wobbled past the heaps of waste he had pushed aside, the door he had sealed just a few hours earlier, the sink of piled, forgotten dishes, the charcoal burning slowly on the stove—to a canvas in the middle of the room.

He stared at it, the blankness of it all taunting him.

Trembling, he picked up his brush—the bristles still crusted with yesterday's colors—and started painting. Even now, as the hours slipped through his grasp, he couldn't stop. He kept reaching for the unreachable. Kept aching for the answers.

Art...

What was art? What was art to him, and what had it become? Those were the questions that echoed in his mind, ceaseless and cruel. They were the questions that had haunted him throughout every phase of life, clinging like unshakable shadows.

Red began to splatter the canvas—maroons and vermillions and carmines staining what had once been blank. He used to paint coquelicot poppies so vivid they danced in the light, yet now the same red was choking the canvas—heavy and unrelenting as it suffocated the easel.

The more he painted, the heavier the air became, the closer the walls seemed to press in.

Each stroke was an obsessive confession.

Each stroke was a loathsome curse.

Art...art...

Art, he thought, was hours of work dismissed by a single scoff. Art was having one-too-many people mock his dreams. Art was the constant labeling of 'useless,' 'naive,' 'yeah, keep dreaming,' and 'go find a real job.' Art was squeezing his eyes shut to tune out such comments, wishing that they would all just *die, die, die.*

Art was realizing—heart twisting with hopelessness—that the skeptics were right. Art was working a dozen part-time jobs with minimum wage to make a living—if one could even call that living. Art was a never-ending turmoil of self-loathing because even he hated his paintings. Art was always despairing, and never being enough. For his family, for the masses, and most of all for himself.

Art. It was a love that had ruined him.

The canvas was now drowning in crimson. It seeped into every centimeter of white, staining it irreparably, just as how his own failures had marred his soul.

His brushstrokes thickened.

His breath thinned.

He dropped his palette.

And yet—his fingers still curled around the brush.

Even as his vision blurred, even as his body trembled, he found himself reaching for the canvas again.

Art…art…art…

Oh, how he hated it.

Yimeng Cai

– Author Interview

Yimeng Cai is a ninth-grade winner of the Inklings Book Contest for her vignette Chiaroscuro. When she's not writing, she can be found painting, playing badminton, or sacrificing sleep over video game pixels. She's passionate about using writing to further test the limits of her own creativity—one draft at a time. She's grateful for the opportunities Young Inklings have provided for her to further grow as a writer.

What books inspire you?

Like many writers, reading is one of my favorite hobbies. However, the more I read, the more cynical I became—picking at the imperfections of every novel, feeling unsatisfied with each read. Perhaps it was the writer in me, ever-so-aware of craft, that made it harder to lose myself in even the most acclaimed stories. Then, my friend recommended *All the Light We Cannot See*—a historical fiction that changed my perspective. I found myself entranced by the writing style, the prose, and the characters. It left me with a sense of satisfaction so many others had not. The book is one of my biggest inspirations when it comes to writing, and I can only dream of one day writing a piece that leaves a reader with half the impact that it left on me.

What inspired your writing journey?

Though many things and people alike have inspired my writing journey, I particularly want to credit two people for my current love for writing: my dear friend and third grade teacher. The latter inspired me to start creative writing in the first place, and the former has been with me through even my worst attempts at 'literature'. However, my inspiration for specific works and pieces are found in seemingly random things—a particularly humid downpour, a newly discovered song, a peculiar dream about talking radishes, and more.

What advice do you have for new writers?

My advice for new writers is let yourself write for you. Don't worry about the possible scrutiny you might face, as you should write for yourself. Write about what your heart desires, even if it may seem like a ludicrous idea. Additionally, my advice for facing writer's block—because so many of us writers have to be faced with this challenge—is simple: take a break. Perhaps that's not the answer some might expect to hear, but burnout—the cause of most of my writing blocks—is more dangerous than it seems. Go outside, touch some grass—and maybe you'll find inspiration in a yellow dandelion blowing away in the wind.

What was it like to advise around a writing strength, rather than a weakness?

Being advised to write around a strength rather than a weakness was certainly new for me. I've always been a perfectionist of sorts, and so a large part of my personal editing process is picking out imperfections in the piece. I suppose it has been eye-opening in a way to focus on the strengths of someone's writing. Yet, that being said, while focusing on strengths is refreshing, I've come to realize that criticism remains invaluable. Without it, weaknesses stagnate. If one only fixates on their strengths and therefore stays ignorant to their flaws, their weaknesses will always stay as weaknesses. Ultimately, while acknowledging one's strengths is important, I still believe that criticism is just as, if not more important. After all, true growth comes from facing our flaws—because only then can we refine them into something remarkable.

52

53

A Satin Pillowcase

by Zoë Friedman

I tried to run miles

So my body would feel heavy enough

My muscles would concave

Into the satin sheets I bought to

Preserve my pretty hair

I tried to practice gratitude

Thank you, Earth, for holding me

For pumping blood into my heart

If you're taking requests

    A little slower, please

I tried to count

All the hours I'd lost

Then down from 100

99

  98

    97

I tried to breathe
Held each breath
For

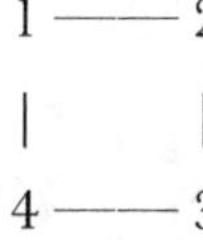

A time signature of panic with
Rests of gasps

I even tried God
When they weren't watching
Sank to my knees
Please God
I know the children
Are starving
And the wars
Devastate
But would you
Spend just a second on me

You won't have anything
To claim
If this keeps up
Just a corpse with
Pretty hair
And a satin pillowcase

Zoë Friedman

– Author Interview

Zoë is entering her senior year at Castilleja School in Palo Alto, California. She is passionate about writing and literature, especially poetry! She was first introduced to the Society of Young Inklings in third grade when she won the 2016 Inklings book competition, sparking her love for creative writing. Zoë is also interested in journalism and serves as the editor of her school paper, as well as an intern at the Los Altos Town Crier. Outside of writing, she enjoys playing lacrosse, singing, and spending time outdoors with friends and family. She is incredibly grateful to everyone at the Society of Young Inklings for their support and encouragement throughout her writing journey.

When did you begin writing, and why?

I began writing in early elementary school, encouraged by phenomenal teachers who nurtured my creativity. Writing quickly became an outlet for me, not just for storytelling and creativity, but for processing my feelings, reflecting on experiences, and observing the world around me. Participating in the Inklings competition in third grade gave me confidence in my abilities and showed me how rewarding writing could be!

What advice do you have for other youth writers?

One of the most important things you can do as a writer is to surround yourself with other creative people who enjoy making art. I really believe that creativity and passion are contagious, and being around people who find beauty and importance in little things will help to inspire your writing.

What inspired this poem?

Before writing this poem, I had been struggling with insomnia and couldn't quite articulate what I was feeling. One day, while on a plane, I began to write and sit with the discomfort and ambiguity in my experience. I found that I needed to write this poem in that moment, as it helped me grapple with what I was going through and gave me a way to process the uncertainty.

What was it like to revise around a writing strength, rather than a weakness?

Focusing my revisions around strengths felt empowering and validating. It was a different experience than one I am used to, and reminded me that revisions can also be about expanding what's already resonating in a piece. Centering my revisions on what felt strong helped preserve my voice and ensured that the poem's truths remained clear throughout the process.

59

His Eyes

by Via M

His eyes still followed mine.

They were a glassy blue, paler than I was used to.

They didn't seem like his eyes.

In my family, the younger sibling always died first. It wasn't some sort of sore subject, it was taken with a grain of salt, especially since we never had any deaths occur prematurely. So then why did I have to see him be buried?

He was just about to graduate.

He had been in the police program for a while.

He was at the top of his class too.

He had always had a heart for helping people. When I was younger, he was the one to bandage my scrapes whenever I fell. He was the one to save his change to take me out for ice cream after a tough test, even though I knew he wanted to buy some new sneakers. He ran a lot, so the ones he had got holes quickly.

I wanted him to be buried with them, but Dad said it was inappropriate, and had him wear the stuffy dress shoes he hated instead.

One of his friends from the police academy noticed too, even taking the time to talk to me while we waited for the body to be carried out.

He used to come over often, and I remember him picking me up from school whenever my brother couldn't. For my birthday, he even bought me a book I had wanted for a while. We haven't talked since the funeral.

I don't think I even remember his name anymore.

—

It's been three weeks since the funeral.

We don't have any family photos hanging on the walls anymore. I think they're wherever Mom put the rest of his stuff.

We don't have family dinners anymore either.

Mom still cries a lot.

Dad stopped a while ago, but I always smell gasoline on his breath when he comes home. Or at least, I tell myself that it's gasoline.

I don't talk to my friends anymore.

It takes too much effort.

I think my friends might be avoiding me too.

I can't blame them though. It must be pretty awkward to try and start a conversation with someone whose brother just got murdered. I'd probably not talk to them either. Or maybe I'd try, but I don't know if it would work.

I don't think I'd be very helpful, or comforting.

That was my brother's thing. If I had caught that bullet instead of him, he would have turned around and started comforting others even if it meant he needed to put his grief on hold. I must be selfish like that, wishing it was me instead of him.

No.

No, I don't wish that.

I just want him back.

——

I heard my mom on the phone this morning.

She was sitting at the kitchen table with a glass of wine in her hands.

Dad was at work, and she probably thought I was at school.

Maybe that was why she had the phone on speaker.

I don't know exactly who she was talking to, but they seemed rude. They were talking about me.

More specifically, my relationship with my brother.

And maybe that's why I stayed and listened, hidden up the stairs. If it was just about me, I wouldn't care.

I could defend myself from her words if I truly wanted to. Mom always talked about me like that anyway.

But she put my brother's name in her mouth as a reason for an excuse. That was crossing a line.

He can't defend himself.

He no longer has a mouth to speak anyway.

"She's been so distant lately."

Mom never talked to me before the accident anyway. "She needs to take responsibility."

Mom's always wine drunk and Dad barely comes home. "If only her brother could see her now."

I was the last one he ever looked at.

"She'll heal in time."

Time itself could not heal.

"It should've been her."

I stopped listening after that.

—

It's been five months, two weeks, and six days since the funeral. Dad moved out.

He met someone at work who made him happy and forgot everything here. For that reason alone, I don't blame him for leaving.

It's not like it hurts anyway.

It's just another fact of life.

Besides, there's nothing I would be able to do even if I wanted to. Mom slipped up and told me my brother's stuff was in the attic. Including the bulletproof vest he was supposed to be wearing that day. She had talked about burning it but was always too drunk to remember. I think that's where she keeps all the pictures too.

I'm too scared to go up and look.

-

It's been one year, seven months, and three days since the funeral. I'm beginning to forget what my brother's face looks like. It's getting more and more tempting to peek into the attic. I want to see his face again.

But Mom keeps it locked, and I don't know where the key is. Maybe another time.

—

It's been exactly three years since the funeral.

Mom's gone.

She's been gone for a while.

Her liver failed, and I can't say I'm surprised.

I knew it was coming.

We had a small funeral for her, nothing like what we gave my brother.

It's my job to clean out the house now.

I found the keys to the attic hidden behind the wedding photo of my parents, which hung above their bed.

It was the day after my brother's anniversary when I unlocked it.

—

It was another two months before I went up there.

I was right.

She had put away all the memories in the attic.

His vest was tucked under Christmas decoration boxes.

The certificate we received on his behalf was eaten away by moths.

His running shoes had become home for mice.

I found the old pictures last, perfectly preserved.

Not a spec of dust.

In those, he was smiling.

His eyes still followed mine.

Via M

– Author Interview

By the age of seventeen, Via M. has already achieved impressive literary milestones, having her short stories published by the St. Louis Writers Guild, Echo Magazine, and Young Inklings' short story competition (now twice!). Alongside her passion for writing, Via cultivated a rich background in theater, showcasing her talents in acting, singing, dancing, stage management, and scriptwriting. She further expanded her creative horizons by attending Webster University's Film Camp twice, as well as their Animation camp where she contributed to short films and produced her own animations. Currently, Via is an active member of her school's journalism team, engaging in anchoring, scripting, video production, and idea development. She serves on her school's ITS executive team, residing in St. Louis, MO. Via M. is represented by Andrea Comparato of Inscriptions Literary. @viamdimensions on Instagram.

What was the editorial process with Inklings like?

The editorial process was easy to follow and rewarding. At the very start, the other writers and I were given a starter pack that included a detailed outline of our deadlines and projects, explaining exactly how to do everything and what to expect. The packet also gave us tips for line editing as well as revision focuses. While most editorial stages I'm used to having basic line notes and theme feedback, something that was very helpful about this approach with Inklings was that we were encouraged to focus on things we were doing well in our writing, and how to carry that throughout pieces of our work. Overall, the editorial process was very helpful in bringing our stories to life.

What are some of your favorite stories/things to draw inspiration from?

I've actually been watching a lot more kdramas and animations. While I still read quite a bit, as I've gotten more interested in script writing and breaking into the film industry, what I draw my inspiration from has greatly changed. One of my biggest inspirations is the kdrama *Bloodhounds*. Not only is the pacing and story done incredibly well, but the character dynamics are truly at the heart of this series. Within just the first few minutes of the two main characters interacting, they immediately become brothers that will do anything for each other. I really can't even begin to describe how much their character dynamic has influenced my own character dynamics across multiple stories! It's truly done in such a way that nothing else really compares. The anime *One Piece* has greatly influenced my world building, as each island the crew travels to is unique and astonishing, each offering quests and challenges only specific to the arc/island. There is never a dull moment.

If your story/poem were to be adapted into another format, what would it be and why?

I think that having my story be adapted into a short comic would be very interesting. Even though I've just gone on and on about film, the actual written words of my story is what really brings the whole thing together. A comic would allow beautiful representation of the narrative, whilst keeping the writing style to a line per panel.

How did you approach writing *His Eyes*?

His Eyes was actually written for a completely different contest that I ended up not entering. That's why the first and last lines are the same, as that was one of the criteria for the contest. The other criteria was that there had to be an overheard conversation and the line "Time itself could not heal".

As far as writing the actual story, I have absolutely no idea where it came from nor any of my thought process when writing. I just kinda blinked and it was written. Usually when I write shorter/self-contained pieces, I choose a song to have on repeat as I write, which usually affects the tone. I'm pretty sure I was listening to *WildFlower* by Billie Ellish since I was writing to that song quite a bit around that time, but I'm not sure. Sometimes our best stories unfold when we don't even mean for them to!

What are some other projects you are currently working on?

I currently have two stories in submission with my agent. One is a novel titled *I've Seen the End* and another is a scripted animated TV show called *Ballad of Fools*. Wish me luck with those! Other than that, I am currently working on a pitch and pilot for another show, as well as working on two other TV show ideas and multiple books.

Any advice to other youth writers?

Just create. It doesn't matter what it is, who it's for, why you're making it - just create. Not only does it help you grow in whatever creative outlet you're pursuing, but it also just makes you happy (or at least it should in most circumstances). Also something to be cautious of is getting stressed out, especially if you're trying to get your work out there professionally. Being creative is supposed to be escapism, to make us experience something that we normally wouldn't and bring us to a place that makes us feel better, learn something new, etc. When

I started bringing my creative work into the professional space, I was very scared, insecure, and impatient. Even though those are things I still greatly struggle with (and probably will for a long time), it is important to not let go of the reason why you started creating in the first place, no matter what that looked like for you personally. Make sure you're creating because YOU want to. It's yours before it's anyone else's.

Extraordinary

by Eleanor Frink-Davis

Extraordinary

I've spent my whole life
Trying to escape the ordinary.
My imagination ran wild within me
Dreaming of talking stuffed animals
And monsters under the bed.
I feared
Yet hoped
My life was special.
Different.
Extraordinary.

I devoured books like they were the nectar of life
Letting them pick me up
And set me down
Somewhere utterly new.
Where a girl like me could harness the elements
A blazing ball of fire in each hand as she learned she could move mountains.
Where she could vanquish armies with only her wits
And a motley crew of friends by her side.

Where she could fulfill prophecies

Or shatter them

Into a million glittering pieces

Ride fierce-eyed dragons, face tilted toward the sun, hair snapping in the breeze.

Where a girl like me

Could be miraculous.

Magical.

Exceptional.

Just a little bit *more*

Than everyone else.

Dear Hogwarts,

I'm still waiting for my letter. I think the owl may have gotten lost crossing the Atlantic.

Regards, Eleanor.

Once I resigned myself to my magicless existence

I took to the stage.

I tried on new personalities like they were secondhand hats

Used by someone else, but no longer quite the same.

I thought I was talented

Maybe even…*extraordinary*.

But pride comes before the fall

And though I didn't fall far

And I didn't fall hard

The bruises were the dark, deep purple of disappointed dreams.

If I want to be extraordinary

Then I must take these hands

This head

This heart

Take these pieces of me, bright and burning with promise

And sculpt them into something spectacular.

And maybe I *do* shine bright

And maybe I'm exceptional

But when does *extraordinary* become *ordinary*?

Of course she's incredible.

That's just who she is.

Of course

She's just a little bit smarter

Than everyone else.

She always has been. Haven't you noticed?

But

Of course

She's ashamed

Because she still isn't perfect.

She knows

And frets

That anything less than the best would be a lesson in surprise

That she refuses to teach.

Her knowing facade

Hides a whirlpool of stress

And a growing cloud of shame

Because maybe

For the first time

She actually *is* extraordinary.

I've spent my whole life

Running from ordinary

Thinking I must be something more

Because, *hello!* I'm *me!*

The ugly duckling was special

But I'm no swan

And these wax-paper wings

Don't know how to fly.

Because even as I strive to be

Extraordinary

Something pulls me back to earth.

Maybe

I don't want to be rude.

Maybe

I don't want to stand out.

Maybe

I just don't want to be…*extraordinary.*

But then again, here I am

Typing on a Google doc in 12 point

Double-spaced

Times New Roman font

Pouring my heart out

To the clacking of the keys

(Especially the backspace.)

Extraordinary

Flexing my fingers
To awaken the ink running through my veins
Straining, struggling, *striving* to create a masterpiece
Hoping that somehow
I can be
Just a little bit better than everyone else.
Special.
Different.
Miraculous.
And maybe
Even
Extraordinary.

Eleanor Frink-Davis

– Author Interview

Hi, I'm Eleanor! I live in Portland, Oregon, and I'm a rising sophomore in high school. When I'm not writing, you can find me curled up on the couch with a book, singing along to my favorite musicals, playing piano, or hanging out with friends at mock trial practice. Some of my favorite books–and it was hard to pick just a few!–are *A Darker Shade of Magic* by V. E. Schwab, *Code Name Verity* by Elizabeth Wein, and *Pride and Prejudice* by Jane Austen. My favorite types of writing are poetry and mysteries because I like planning things out.

What inspired your piece?

"Extraordinary" is a mix of a lot of different emotions. It centers around the feeling of wanting to be special. I'm a super competitive person, so I always feel like I need a "thing" to be the best at. On the other hand, I actually am good at a lot of things and this leads to perfectionism and stress. I worry that if I mess up, I'll let people down. Then there's the conflicting urge to blend in, because I worry that others will feel bad. It's like the things I'm good at are the things I want to be average at, and the things I'm average at I want to be good at. My poem combines these conflicting emotions to show my fluctuation between wanting to blend in and wanting to be extraordinary.

What was the main thing you were looking for in revision?

Well, I was taking pictures of the poem to text to my friend and I noticed that it was eight pages long! I really hadn't noticed how long it was before then, so it was a bit of an eye-opener. There were also a lot of phrases that seemed out of place or clunky that I wanted to edit or completely take out. With these two things in mind, I chose word choice as my revision focus. I zeroed in on making sure every word and every line was there for a reason and sounded the best it could be. If I didn't like something, I'd add a comment that just said "ehh" or "no" and come back to it later with fresh eyes. By the end of my revisions, my poem felt a lot more smooth and streamlined. I also managed to cut 200 words!

What advice do you have for other young writers?

My main piece of advice is to simply get words on the page. It can be difficult to shake off perfectionism, but if you can find a way to ignore your inner critic and just write, that'll be super helpful. Nothing has to be perfect the first time! Similarly, separate your writing from your editing. I find that if I try to edit while I write, I'll lose my train of thought or end up with nothing at all. I like to set word count goals for myself as motivation to keep writing because even if I write badly, it's still somewhere to start. It's way easier to edit and improve a hundred iffy words than it is to edit and improve nothing at all. Think of your first-draft writing as a placeholder, because that's what it is. It's meant to be imperfect, because you're meant to come back later and read it and stare at it and fix it and then throw half of it out anyway. That's how writing works. It took me a long time to grasp this, and I wish I'd figured it out sooner!

Obsolescence

by Naomi Pond

A year had passed since I had been stationed in Hartley Central Library. It was 2063: the last of the paper books hadn't yet been digitized; the last of the old buildings hadn't yet been torn down. I knew the history of the libraries, all that there was to know. From Ashurbanipal to Alexandria to the abundant public collections of the early twenty-first century, I was well aware of all that had come before this place—I liked to think that knowledge made me particularly qualified to work here, but none of our patrons seemed to care when I explained that to them.

Only one or two visitors besides Matthew, the head librarian, and me, one of an ever-changing string of assistants who were inevitably subject to restructuring, were in the building at the time, and watching their slow movements and occasional page flips was my only entertainment. On the off chance one of the patrons had a question that couldn't be answered by the helper bots stationed in front of me, I was confined to the front desk with nothing to do but filter through the personal data collected on earlier visitors and sort it for our files.

Matthew was wandering through the tall shelves in front of me, stumbling around in search of a book someone had put on hold that morning. He'd been looking for nearly fifteen minutes now, and behind the thick frames of his glasses, his face looked slack and vacant. "Are you alright, Matthew?"

Sometimes he needed a bit of a reminder of where he was, what he was supposed to be doing. The monotony of the job seemed as if it would drive anyone crazy in time, and if Matthew's white hair and deep wrinkles were any indication, he had been working there for decades at that point.

Matthew often messed with the bots when he thought no one else was around, requesting book after book and watching them get pulled from the shelves until there were too many for the poor things to carry and they spilled out all across the floor. They were older models, still susceptible to such antics—perhaps that was why Matthew hadn't replaced them for so many years despite cycling through new personal assistants so quickly. He got some satisfaction from picking the books back up, I suppose, reshelving piles and piles of them as if he were one of the librarians from the twenties, back when people actually checked out books in such numbers.

My voice seemed to free Matthew from the trance he was under. His back straightened out again, and he smoothed his rumpled flannel shirt. He walked with purpose towards the fiction section, reaching a wrinkled hand to pull out the book before returning to the desk.

I suppose that was what my real job was meant to be—to keep Matthew attentive, to ensure that he didn't stay lost for too long. The work certainly wouldn't be too much for him on his own, if only he had the presence of mind to do it.

"Found it," he said, showing the novel to me.

It was a fantasy, its cover bright and colorful with looping text. I had never read it, for I was still making my way through the seemingly never ending backlog of dystopian novels written earlier this century. The darkness and corruption that filled past generations' projections of the future never failed to shock me. Still, they made me feel pleased with how the present had turned out—at least what little I was able to see of it—and grateful that Matthew and I could do our part to preserve this pocket of the past.

I pulled up the person who had placed the hold on my screen, and I recognized the face that stared back at me from the computer. She was a teenage girl, and she wore the regulation

blue uniform for students in our area. We had just approved the issue of her library card a couple hours ago. Sixteen and finally using the library for the first time.

Shoulders slumping, I pushed the button to notify her that the hold was ready. The girl was probably just doing this for an assignment—we rarely got visitors so young for any other purpose these days.

The helper bots could have done this for me, of course. Their interface, while simplistic, was certainly advanced enough to do these tasks in my stead. Still, I liked to feel useful when I could.

The hold found and the girl alerted, our list of things to do that day was complete. Matthew stared at me vacantly, only rounding the corner of the desk to the chair by my side when I waved a hand in front of his face.

"The delivery's coming today," he reminded me, as if the thought of it hadn't been filling the storage in my mind all week.

As he sat down next to me, he actually looked happy, decidedly more so than he had earlier that day.

I saw no purpose in responding. The package would arrive soon enough; we could discuss it then.

Matthew tapped his fingers on my desk anxiously, then ran one hand through his fine white hair. He clearly was waiting for me to say something to break the silence, but I did not want to talk to him. Ordinarily, I tried to be better company, but today I did not trust myself to say more than a few words.

Searching for a way to distract myself, I lifted the dystopian novel that Matthew had last recommended I read, admiring the way the fluorescent lights above shone on the cover, reflecting a warped image of my face back to me. I picked up where I left off, rapidly losing myself in its world. While I certainly did not live under as much persecution as the book's citizens seemed to, I took comfort in seeing others like me, made to stay within the walls of their city—or in my case, within the Hartley Central branch—despite dreams of exploring elsewhere.

After a few minutes of quiet, punctuated only by the flip of my novel's page every few seconds, our last remaining customer left, having decided not to check anything out—whatever they wanted could be found online, anyway.

"Have a nice day!" I said automatically as the doors slid closed, voice cheerful and bright. I did not feel cheerful.

We sat for a while longer, and Matthew's eyelids began to droop, his glasses sliding down his long nose. After some time, a ping echoed from my screen, the sound harsh against the silence, and his eyes shot back open. I put my book down, my world shrinking back to the contents of these four walls.

"It is here," I alerted Matthew. I did not want to tell him, but I had no choice but to follow the protocol.

He heaved himself upwards, bracing his arm against the desk as he circled it and approached the door. Both of the helper bots followed, their wheels whirring against the carpeted floor, ready to help him lift the box, and I was left alone.

The silence was far more complete now that they had departed. The ambient sounds of Matthew breathing, his clothes rustling, the bots' fans running—all were gone. It was only a few moments, though, before the door slid back open, allowing a beam of sunlight to fall inside as Matthew and the bots, carrying a large cardboard box, returned. I craned my head towards the light, trying to catch a last glimpse of the world outside, but the doors rolled shut before I could see.

The bots deposited the box on my desk, then returned to their positions. It was rectangular, about half Matthew's height if it had been turned vertically, and looked quite heavy. Something inside me twisted as I saw it, and I leaned away as far as I could manage in my chair.

With no hesitation, Matthew ripped open the tape, opening the wide flaps to pull out a thick manual.

"JUNE 2063 MODEL: Emotions lessened for improved workplace behavior," he read approvingly. "Same great compliance, now with less existential dread!"

As he went through the manual, nodding with admiration at each listed improvement, I was silent. When Matthew reached the end of the large print, he turned to look at me, a wide smile stretching over his face. I mimicked the behavior, though I did not feel like smiling.

"Why don't you take it out?" Matthew asked, magnanimously gesturing to the box.

A layer of cream-colored foam cushioning covered what was inside. I reached forwards, hands moving on instinct, and pulled it away, laying it carefully on my table. I looked back at the box.

My own face stared back.

Slight changes had been made, of course. Their smile was wider and more genuine, the corners of their gently closed eyes were crinkled. I did not want to look at them, but I did. My gaze did not waver from their friendly face, their perfect skin, as Matthew reached for the power button at the back of their head.

Their eyes opened, and the corners of their mouth turned further upwards. "Hello, Matthew. I am eager to work with you."

Matthew had turned from me now, his deep gaze fixed on my replacement. "And I with you."

The bot reached upwards, offering a hand for Matthew to shake. I had not done that a year ago, when I had first arrived. It must have been another new update; Matthew seemed pleased by the gesture.

"Take them away," he called to the helper bots, still not looking at me.

I did not want to go.

The two buzzed towards me and lifted me from my seat, detaching the wires that linked me at the hips to my rotating office chair. I was dropped unceremoniously into a waiting box, and the same sheet of smooth foam was placed over the bottom half of my face.

I was never taught how to say goodbye. There was protocol for this, of course—what words I was meant to say, what gestures I was meant to make— but there was no training data instructing me on how to feel.

I suppose that was what they sought to remove in the new model. No emotions meant no struggle to comprehend all of this, no hard feelings when the next edition came around, nothing but apathy no matter what happened. Perhaps that was why Matthew always seemed so distant from me—with new assistants arriving annually, he had grown used to earlier models with far less feeling. It was like my books always said; it took humans ages to truly accept new technology. Matthew had simply been too old to adapt, and so he saw me not as a partner but as another in a long string of servants. I couldn't blame him for that—it was simply a flaw in how he was built.

The motors within my neck hummed softly as I turned towards Matthew, his figure haloed by the fluorescent lighting above us.

"Goodbye, Matthew," I said, voice muffled beneath the foam covering it.

The protocol did not specify what volume I was meant to use, and so I was quiet. I doubted that he could hear me—his ears were not calibrated to handle noises so low—but if he did, he did not turn to me.

Above, the bots seemed to be awaiting his instruction. They waited there, spindly arms stretched out and hovering inches away from the power button on the back of my neck. I wondered if I would have run from them if I had legs. I did not want to leave the library, for it was all that I knew. But I did not want to stay here, silent, waiting for everything to end. I had always thought it was foolish when I read of humans with hopes of their souls surviving after death, but now, I couldn't help but wish that I would have the capacity to do the same, that my mind would not be wiped before I was sent off to my next task like every other assistant I had read about. There were so many books still to read, so much still to see in every microscopic movement that the humans made, every breath that they took, every time that Matthew smiled at some far-off memory and the creases in his face smoothed, if only for a brief moment.

No, I decided, *even if I had the power to do so, I would not have tried to escape.*

I knew nothing but this library, nothing but its history. I was simply powered on at the start of the day and off at the end of it, never catching even a glimpse of what may lie beyond. I did not know where I would go from here or what was done with bots who, like me, had completed the work we had been designated to do. I did not know why they continued to send assistants to Matthew, why he needed the newest model to ensure that he continued to do his job, why I was not enough. All I knew was that I had no other role but to sit in my chair and watch and listen and help Matthew and ensure that this place was able to live on and share its stories with those who still needed them.

Perhaps it was simply how I was created, but I could think of no purpose more valuable than the one I had already been able to fulfill. Looking towards him, towards my books and my chair and the room that was all I had known, I smiled. For the first time today, I truly wanted to.

"I will miss you," I whispered, this time speaking loud enough for Matthew to hear it.

He turned to face me, looking down at me through bushy white eyebrows.

"I hope…" he began, words cutting off haltingly.

He blinked three times rapidly, and his soft smile wavered. It looked as if his face were about to collapse inwards. I had never seen him in this state before—the closest match that my image recognition could find to his expression was that of a seven year old boy who had visited Hartley Central three weeks earlier, his bottom lip trembling before he burst into tears. My visual sensors zoomed in on Matthew's face as I wondered if he would do the same, if he felt as much sentiment towards me as that little boy did towards the ice cream he had cried over that afternoon.

But before I could tell, Matthew turned away, shoulders stiffening.

"I'm sorry."

He signaled to one of the helper bots.

Face blank, the bot reached around the side of my neck and pressed the button, powering me off.

Naomi Pond
– Author Interview

Naomi Pond is a homeschooled high schooler who lives in Irvine, California with her parents, two dogs, and a perhaps excessive number of books. She hopes to become a librarian and author when she grows up, and she currently spends much of her time volunteering at her local library and brainstorming new short stories. While she usually focuses on shorter fiction, she is also working on the second draft of her novel *Lost Woods*, a dystopian/fantasy based on her short story in the 2022 Inklings Book.

What inspired your piece?

"Obsolescence" was in large part inspired by the time I've spent volunteering at my local library. I plan to be a librarian when I grow up, and if I succeed at that goal, I will actually be working in a library in 2063 at a similar age to Matthew in my story! At the same time, I have been doing a lot of research about how technology will affect the libraries and reading habits of the future and watching with quite a bit of concern as generative AI and technological replacements for physical books and materials become increasingly convincing and commonplace. All of these ideas managed to fit together quite well into my story, and I hope that it will inspire others to consider these topics and the extent to which AI and other recent technologies threaten creativity and human relationships.

How did you approach writing "Obsolescence?"

My process with this story turned out to be very different from many others that I've written. I have always seen myself as a meticulous planner—I love brainstorming detailed settings, answering hundred-question long character questionnaires, and creating spreadsheets to map out the plot. However, "Obsolescence" was very different. The story began with a fifteen-minute exercise at the beginning of my dual enrollment creative writing class, and I couldn't stop thinking about it for the rest of the night. It was a few days before I had the time to continue with the piece, but I ended up writing the entire 1000-word first draft in a single sitting and then expanding it to nearly double the length over the following week. Unlike most of my previous stories, I haven't done much concrete development of the characters and the setting outside what is written in the piece itself, though I have completed a few shorter pieces focusing on the same characters since then. I'm not sure where I will go next with this story, but its world has certainly stuck with me even months following its creation!

What was something surprising you learned while editing?

While I was pretty satisfied with the ending of my story when I submitted it to the contest, it unexpectedly ended up being where the majority of my revision was focused. I added several paragraphs to the concluding page to better emphasize the relationship between my two characters and hint towards further feelings, and I'm really pleased with the new material that I uncovered during the process. Definitely don't skip to the end when you're reading, though, I promise it'll be worth the wait! :)

What advice do you have for other young authors?

Take advantage of all of the opportunities that you can! While it may seem like the reverse is true sometimes, there are so many things that you have access to as a young author that may not be quite so easy for adults. Along with the Inklings Book Contest, plenty of literary journals, anthologies, and contests are seeking work specifically by young people, and there is little standing in your way when submitting to them. It might seem scary to put your work—and yourself—out into the world, but there are few drawbacks and so many benefits that doing so is almost always worth a shot.

www.ingramcontent.com/pod-product-compliance
Lightning Source LLC
Chambersburg PA
CBHW071950190726
48293CB00004B/1415